SAN FRANCISCO Giants

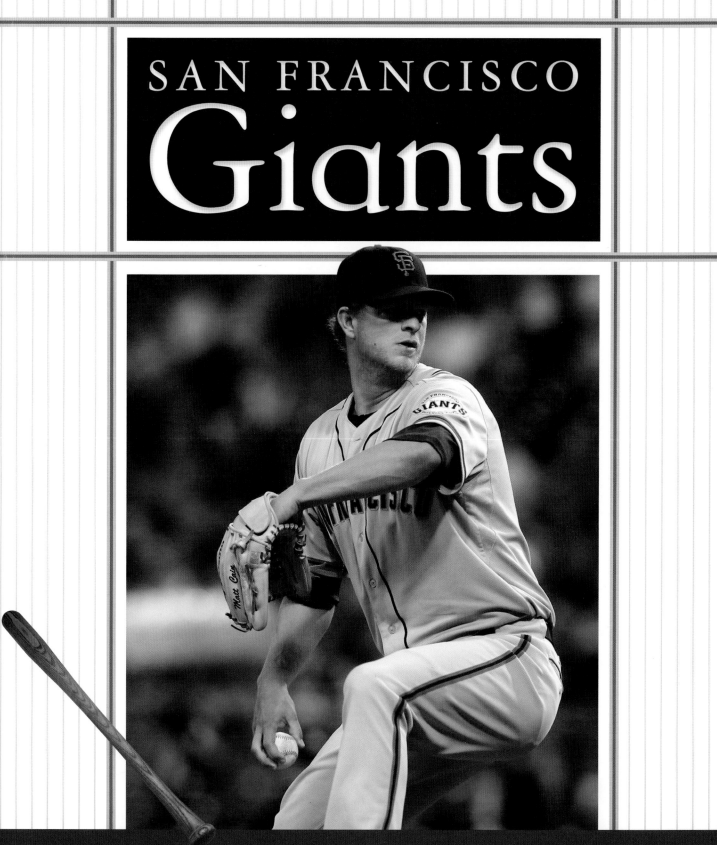

BY ALEX MONNIG

The Child's World®

Published by The Child's World®
1980 Lookout Drive • Mankato, MN 56003-1705
800-599-READ • www.childsworld.com

Acknowledgments
The Child's World®: Mary Berendes, Publishing Director
Red Line Editorial: Editorial direction
The Design Lab: Design
Amnet: Production
Design Elements: Photodisc

Photographs ©: Keith Srakocic/AP Images, cover, 1, 2; Brian Murphy/Icon SMI, 5, 6; Public Domain, 9; Cal Sport Media/AP Images, 10; Eric Broder Van Dyke/Shutterstock Images, 13, 25 (center); Design Lab, 14; Kyodo/AP Images, 17; Susan Ragan/AP Images, 18; Marcio Jose Sanchez/AP Images, 21; ZUMA Press/Icon SMI, 22; AP Images, 22 (inset); Mark LoMoglio/Icon SMI, 25 (top), 26; Photo Works/Shutterstock Images, 25 (bottom); Juan DeLeon/Icon SMI, 27

ISBN 9781623239787
LCCN 2013947290

Printed in the United States of America
Mankato, MN
December, 2013
PA02188

ABOUT THE AUTHOR

Alex Monnig is a journalist who has covered sporting events around the world and written more than a dozen sports books for young readers. Even though he is sometimes far from home, he always follows his favorite team, the St. Louis Cardinals.

Cover: Matt Cain, Pitcher

CONTENTS

Go, Giants!

The San Francisco Giants are one of baseball's oldest and most successful franchises. They have built a large fan base across the country throughout their rich history. They have appeared in the **World Series** 18 times. That is more than any other team besides the New York Yankees! The team has been especially good in recent years. Let's meet the Giants!

Buster Posey (left) congratulates pitcher Sergio Romo after another Giants victory.

Who Are the Giants?

The San Francisco Giants are a team in baseball's National League (NL). The NL joins with the American League (AL) to form Major League Baseball. The Giants play in the West Division of the NL. The division winners and two wild-card teams get to play in the league playoffs. The playoff winners from the two leagues face off in the World Series. The Giants have won seven World Series championships.

Marco Scutaro follows through on his swing in a game against the Milwaukee Brewers.

Where They Came From

The Giants have not always played their games in San Francisco. In fact, they were not always called the Giants. The team started in 1883 as the New York Gothams. In 1885, they became the New York Giants. Before the 1958 season, the team moved to San Francisco to become the Giants everybody knows today.

The 1884 New York Gothams team posing for their team photo.

Who They Play

The San Francisco Giants play 162 games each season. That includes about 19 games against each of the other teams in their division. The Giants have won eight NL West championships. The other NL West teams are the Arizona Diamondbacks, the Colorado Rockies, the Los Angeles Dodgers, and the San Diego Padres. The Giants and the Dodgers are two of baseball's biggest **rivals**. Their games always get the fans charged up! Both of these teams moved from New York to California. The Giants also play some teams from the AL. Their AL opponents change every year.

Shortstop Brandon Crawford tags a Dodgers player out at second base.

Where They Play

AT&T Park is home of the San Francisco Giants. The stadium holds about 41,000 fans. It has hosted many memorable events since opening on April 11, 2000. One of the best parts of the stadium is McCovey Cove. It is named after legendary Giants first baseman Willie McCovey. Home runs fly over the right field wall and land with a splash in the water directly behind the stadium. Then people in kayaks race to grab them as souvenirs!

McCovey Cove fills with Giants fans in kayaks and boats during games.

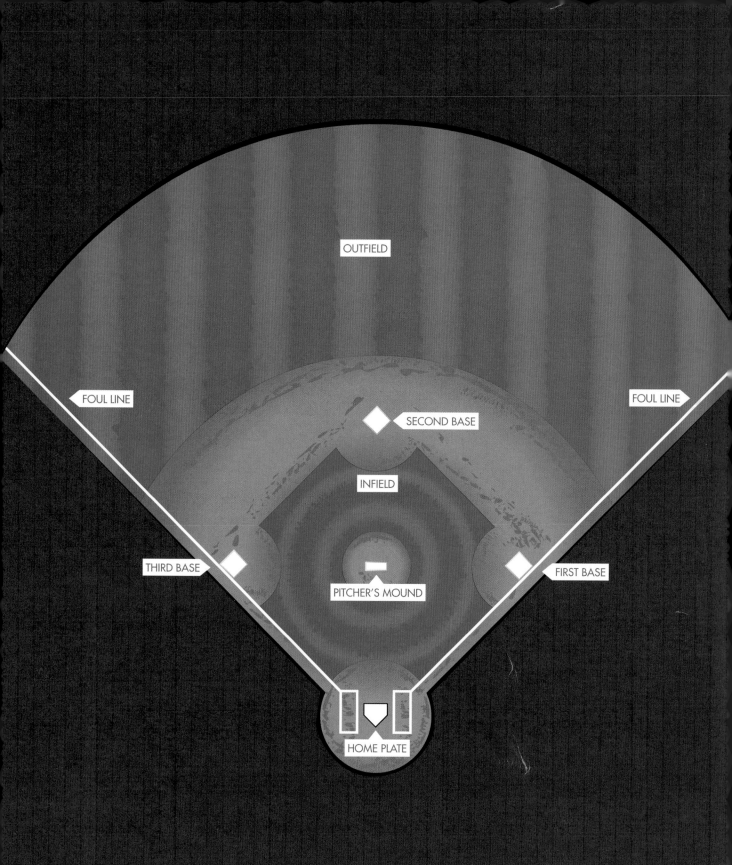

OUTFIELD

FOUL LINE

FOUL LINE

SECOND BASE

INFIELD

THIRD BASE

FIRST BASE

PITCHER'S MOUND

HOME PLATE

The Baseball Diamond

Baseball games are played on a field called a diamond. Four bases form this diamond shape. The bases are 90 feet (27 m) apart. The area around and between the bases is called the infield. At the center of the infield is the pitcher's mound. The grass area beyond the bases is called the outfield. White lines start at **home plate** and go toward the outfield. These are the foul lines. Baseballs hit outside these lines are out of play unless they are caught by a fielder. The outfield walls are about 300–450 feet (91–137 m) from home plate.

Big Days

The Giants have had some great seasons in their history. Here are three of the greatest:

1905: *The Giants won 105 games, one less than the team record set in 1904, and won their first World Series title.*

2010: *The wait was finally over! The Giants won their first World Series since 1954 by beating the Texas Rangers in five games.*

2012: *Led by great pitching, San Francisco did it again, overcoming a three-games-to-one deficit against the St. Louis Cardinals in the National League Championship Series before defeating the Detroit Tigers for another World Series crown.*

Giants players celebrate on the field after winning the 2012 World Series against the Tigers.

Tough Days

Even the successful San Francisco Giants go through bad seasons and tough times. Here are some of the biggest disappointments in Giants history:

1962: *The Giants scratched out just four hits and lost Game 7 of the World Series 1–0 to the New York Yankees.*

1985: *This was a season San Francisco fans would like to forget. The Giants missed the playoffs for the 14th straight season and set a team record by losing 100 games.*

1993: *San Francisco entered the final day of the season tied for first in the NL West with the Atlanta Braves. If both teams won, they would play each other to decide who made the playoffs. The Braves did their part, but the Giants got smashed 12–1 by the rival Los Angeles Dodgers and missed out.*

Giants players can't watch as their playoff hopes slip away in 1993.

Meet the Fans

Giants fans are not afraid to use different props to show how much they love their team. During the playoffs, fans wave orange towels to support their team. Others will wear panda hats in honor of third baseman Pablo "Kung Fu Panda" Sandoval! Even when it gets cold next to the San Francisco Bay, loyal fans show up in full force to cheer on the Giants. **Mascot** Lou Seal helps get people fired up to support the team.

Giants fans show their support for their favorite team.

Willie Mays, Outfield

Heroes Then . . .

Pitcher Christy Mathewson played for the Giants from 1900 to 1916 and was one of the first five players ever inducted into the Hall of Fame. Outfielder Mel Ott was one of the first great power hitters to step onto the diamond. Outfielder Willie Mays was an **All Star** an incredible 19 years in a row from 1954 to 1972. He won two **Most Valuable Player (MVP)** awards and smacked 660 home runs in his career. Willie McCovey hit 521 home runs mostly during the 1960s and 1970s. Some say outfielder Barry Bonds is the best player ever. He won five of his record seven MVP awards with the Giants. He also broke the single-season home run record when he crushed 73 home runs in 2001. He retired in 2007 with 762 home runs, the most in history. **Manager** John McGraw retired with an amazing 2,583 wins for the Giants.

Barry Bonds was one of the greatest power hitters of all time.

Heroes Now . . .

Young catcher Buster Posey won the Rookie of the Year Award in 2010 before breaking his leg in a collision at home plate in 2011. But he came back strong in 2012, winning the NL MVP Award and helping the Giants capture another World Series. Ace Matt Cain is consistently in the top ten in innings pitched each year. And lefty Madison Bumgarner is one of the best young hurlers in the game. Manager Bruce Bochy helped lead the Giants to two World Series in his first six years in charge.

The present-day Giants are loaded with star players.

Buster Posey, Catcher

Matt Cain, Pitcher

Madison Bumgarner, Pitcher

BATTING HELMET

BAT

BATTING GLO[VE]

TEAM JERSEY

TEAM PANTS

BASEBALL CLEATS

Gearing Up

Baseball players all wear a team jersey and pants. They have to wear a team hat in the field and a helmet when batting. Take a look at Brandon Belt and Buster Posey to see some other parts of a baseball player's uniform.

CATCHER'S MASK

CATCHER'S MITT

CATCHER'S CHEST PROTECTOR

CATCHER'S SHIN GUARD

Buster Posey, Catcher

On the left: Brandon Belt, First Base

Sports Stats

Here are some all-time career records for the San Francisco Giants. All the stats are through the 2013 season.

THE BASEBALL

A Major League baseball weighs about 5 ounces (142 g). It is 9 inches (23 cm) around. A leather cover surrounds hundreds of feet of string. That string is wound around a small center of rubber and cork.

HOME RUNS

Willie Mays, 646
Barry Bonds, 586

RUNS BATTED IN

Mel Ott, 1,860
Willie Mays, 1,859

BATTING AVERAGE

Bill Terry, .341

George Davis, .332

STOLEN BASES

Mike Tiernan, 428

George Davis, 354

WINS BY A PITCHER

Christy Mathewson, 372

Carl Hubbell, 253

WINS BY A MANAGER

John McGraw, 2,583

EARNED RUN AVERAGE

Christy Mathewson, 2.12

Joe McGinnity, 2.38

Glossary

All Star when a player is selected to play in a yearly game between the best players in each league. Outfielder Willie Mays was an All Star 19 years in a row.

home plate a five-sided rubber pad where batters stand to swing. Runners touch home plate to score runs.

manager the person in charge of the team and who chooses who will bat and pitch. Manager John McGraw retired with the second highest amount of wins in baseball history.

mascot a person in costume or an animal that helps fans cheer for their team. Lou Seal is the Giants' mascot.

Most Valuable Player (MVP) a yearly award given to the top player in each league. Outfielder Willie Mays won two MVP awards.

rivals teams that play each other often and have an ongoing competition. The Giants and the Dodgers are two of baseball's biggest rivals.

World Series the Major League Baseball championship. The World Series is played each year between the winners of the American and National Leagues.

Find Out More

BOOKS

Bay Area News Group. *Comeback Kings: The San Francisco Giants' Incredible 2012 Championship Season.* Chicago, IL: Triumph Books, 2012.

Buckley, James Jr. *Eyewitness Baseball.* New York: DK Publishing, 2010.

Stewart, Mark. *San Francisco Giants.* Chicago, IL: Norwood House Press, 2012.

Teitelbaum, Michael. *Baseball.* Ann Arbor, MI: Cherry Lake Publishing, 2009.

WEB SITES

Visit our Web page for links about the San Francisco Giants and other pro baseball teams. *www.childsworld.com/links*

Note to Parents, Teachers, and Librarians: We routinely verify our Web links to make sure they are safe and active sites. So encourage your readers to check them out!

Index